Dear Parents,

The easy-to-read books in this series are based on The Puzzle Place™, public television's highly praised new show for children that teaches not ABC's or 123's, but "human being" lessons!

In these books, your child will learn about getting along with children from all different backgrounds, about dealing with problems, and making decisions—even when the best thing to do is not always so clear.

Filled with humor, the stories are about situations which all kids face. And best of all, kids can read them all on their own, building a sense of independence and pride.

So come along to the place where it all happens. Come along to The Puzzle Place™....

Copyright © 1996 by Lancit Copyright Corporation/KCET. All rights reserved. Published by Grosset & Dunlap, Inc., a member of The Putnam & Grosset Group, New York. GROSSET & DUNLAP is a trademark of Grosset & Dunlap, Inc. THE PUZZLE PLACE and THE PUZZLE PLACE logo are trademarks of Lancit Media Productions, Ltd. and KCET. Published simultaneously in Canada. Printed in the U.S.A. Library of Congress Catalog Card Number: 96-76134

ISBN 0-448-41312-4 A B C D E F G H I J

The Puzzle Place™ is a co-production of Lancit Media Productions, Ltd., and KCET/Los Angeles. Major funding provided by the Corporation for Public Broadcasting and Edison International.

DON'T CALL ME NAMES!

By Jennifer Dussling
Illustrated by Tom Brannon

Based on the teleplay, "Tippy Woo,"
by John Semper, Susan Amerikaner,
Ellis Weiner, and Tom Dunsmuir.

GROSSET & DUNLAP • NEW YORK

Skye is making a picture
at school.
He has blue paint on his nose...
on his hands...
in his hair.

But Skye is happy.
The picture is
for his grandfather.
He is coming to visit soon.

Bobby sees the blue paint
all over Skye.
"Look!" Bobby says.
"It's Blue Skye!
Get it?
<u>Blue</u> Skye!"

"Very funny," Skye says.

At lunch,

Skye sits next to Mary.

He eats his soup
and his sandwich.
Then he starts to eat his pie.

"How is your Skye Pie?"

Mary giggles.

Skye puts down his fork.

"Ha! Ha!" he says.

But he does not think

it is so funny.

After lunch,
Skye walks slowly back to class.
Why do kids make jokes
about his name?
He has always liked his name.
His grandfather says
it is the best name in the world.
But now Skye is not so sure.

Then Skye sees something
on the wall.
His teacher has hung up
his painting!

But what is that
at the bottom?
Someone has put
the word "Cloudy"
right before his name.
Cloudy Skye!
That does it!

Skye marches off to
The Puzzle Place
with the picture.
He is mad.
But he has an idea.

"Hi, Skye," Leon says.

"My name is not Skye,"
Skye tells him.

"I have a new name.
It's...Jim!"

"But why?" Kiki asks.

"The kids at school
make jokes about my name,"
he says.

He shows them the picture.
"They call me Blue Skye
and Cloudy Skye and Skye Pie."

Kiki nods her head.
"Kids make jokes about
my name, too.
They call me Kooky Kiki!
Don't let it bug you."

But Skye is still mad.
"From now on
    I want to be called Jim,"
he says.
"Okay…<u>Jim</u>," Ben says.

After a while,
the telephone rings.
It is for Skye.
"I'm sorry," Julie says.
"Skye is not here."

Skye acts like he does not care.
But he still wonders
who was on the phone.

Then Jody walks by.
She has something in her hand.
"I found Skye's necklace
  in the other room," she says.
"Too bad he is not here."

Skye frowns.
Maybe this new name
is not such a good idea.

"But my grandfather
gave me that necklace,"
says Skye.
"It is very special!"

Skye stops.

He thinks for a minute.

His grandfather gave him

his <u>name</u>, too.

"I guess my name is
special, too," he says.
"And I guess...
my name is Skye.
Not Jim."

"Well that's good,"
Julie says.
"Because that was
your grandfather
on the phone and..."

DING! DONG!

The doorbell rings.

And who do you think

is there?

Skye's grandfather!